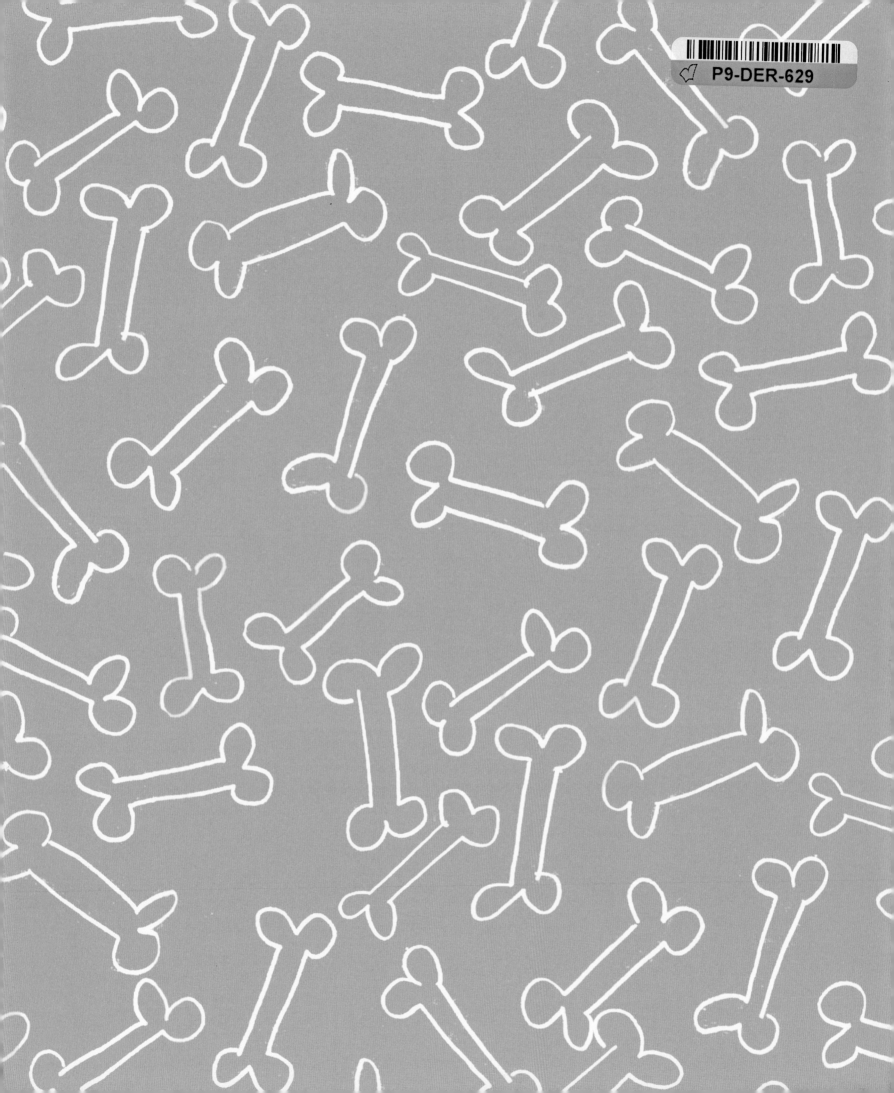

ÉGALITÈ

Bow Wow Meow
Egalité Series

© Text: Blanca Lacasa, 2016
© Illustrations: Gómez, 2016
© Edition: NubeOcho, 2017
www.nubeocho.com – info@nubeocho.com

Original title: *Ni guau ni miau*
Translators: Kim Griffin and Ben Dawlatly
Text editing: Caroline Dookie

Distributed in the United States by
Consortium Book Sales & Distribution

First edition: 2017
ISBN: 978-84-945415-7-5
Printed in China

BOW WOW MEOW

BLANCA LACASA

ILLUSTRATED BY GÓMEZ

nubeOCHO

This is the story of Fabio.

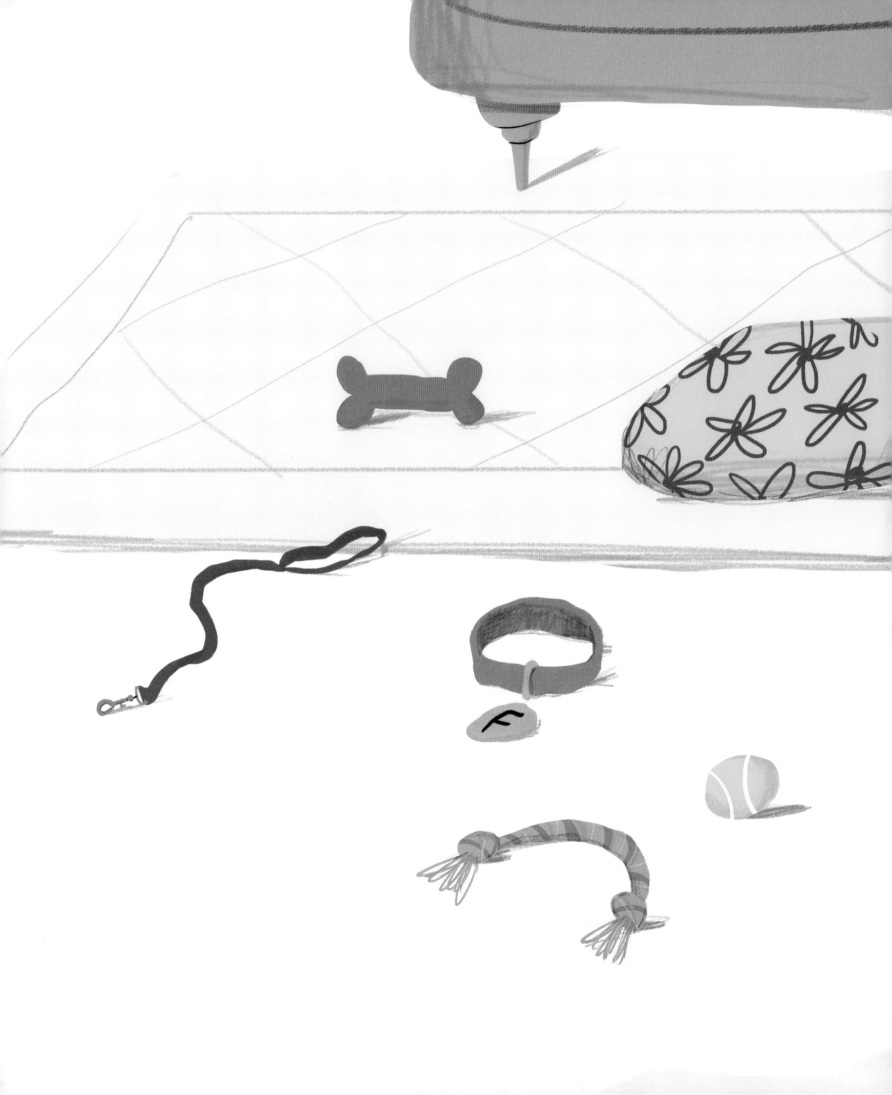

Fabio is a little dog.

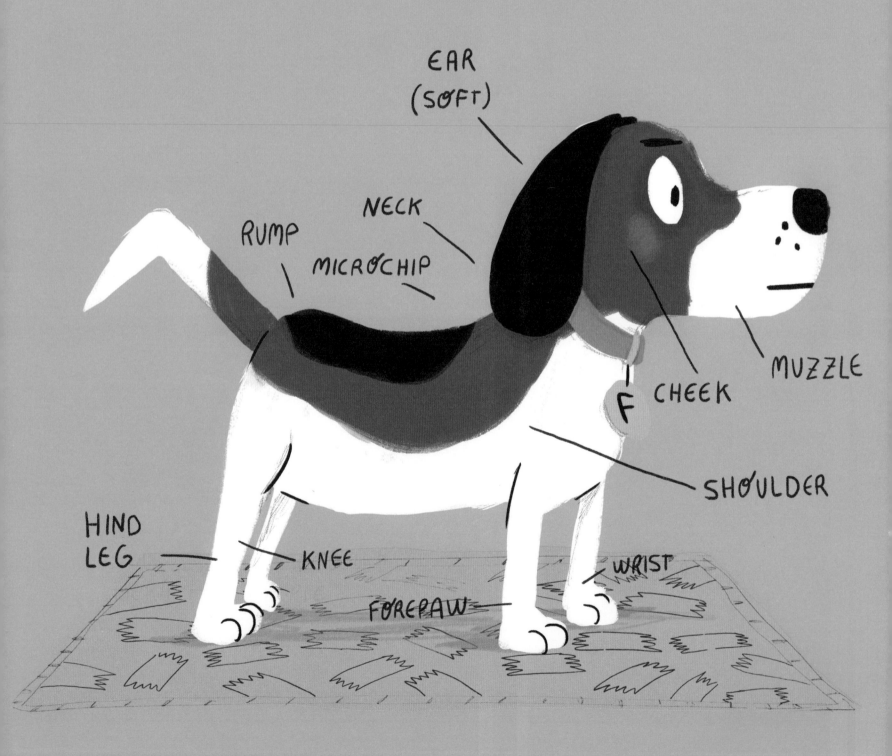

Fabio doesn't play fetch.

Fabio doesn't bark.

Fabio doesn't roll over
to have his belly tickled.

Fabio doesn't
even wag his
little tail.

Fabio doesn't stick his tongue out and pant when he's worn out,

because Fabio doesn't run after sticks.

And he doesn't chase balls either.

Fabio doesn't do anything
that other dogs do.

But Fabio's family still barks at him. They still toss sticks for him, they tickle his belly, they roll around on the floor to play with him, and they still try throwing balls for him to chase…

"Bow-wow!" shouts the little boy, Max.

"Bow-wow!" Max tries again.

But Fabio just stares back silently, looking rather puzzled.

Then one night, Max, with his mouth as dry as a bone, gets out of bed to pour himself a glass of water. It's dark, but he can tell that Fabio, the little dog that doesn't bark, is nowhere to be found…

"That's weird", thinks Max, "It's the middle of the night and Fabio is not curled up somewhere in the house…"

And night after night, it's always the same.

Every time Max hops out of bed, Fabio has performed a vanishing act.

Gone. As if by magic.

One day, Max, who's a brave young boy, stays awake to find out what's going on.

That's when he realizes that Fabio, the little dog who doesn't wag his little tail, sneaks out of the house at night.

Max discovers that his little dog goes out
every night to meet up with a bunch of cats...
cats that definitely do things that other cats do.

Fabio, the special little dog,

sharpens his claws,

climbs up
drainpipes,

chases mice…

Fabio gets tangled up in balls of yarn,

he jumps from rooftops,

and he climbs up trees…

Fabio even bow-wow-meows
(something like a howl crossed
with a meow).

BOWWOWMEOWWW

Every night he meets up with his kitty pals to do
what all cats of the world do:

whatever they please!

From his hiding place, Max keeps a keen eye on his dog. Fabio looks so happy!

After a while, Max walks home slowly, treading softly, lost in thought.

The next morning, everything is the same as usual. Mom greets Fabio with a couple of loud "bow-wows."

BOW WOW

Dad, in turn, says "good morning" with his absolute best impression of a dog.

Nothing works.
Nothing seems to grab poor little Fabio's attention.

Until along comes Max and, without giving it a second thought, he fills up a dish with milk while bow-wow-meowing softly so no one else can hear him.

All of a sudden, Fabio leaps to his feet and looks up at Max with eyes as wide as dinner plates.

Fabio starts to purr and rubs his head against Max's legs.

Max smiles.
Fabio is happy…

At last!